White Bead Ceremony

by
Sherrin Watkins

Illustrated by Kim Doner

Council Oak Books Tulsa Oklahoma

The Greyfeather Series

Council Oak Publishing Co., Inc.
1350 East 15th Street
Tulsa, OK 74120

First edition
Printed in Hong Kong
98 97 96 95 94   5 4 3 2 1

Library of Congress Cataloging-in-Publication Data

Watkins, Sherrin, 1954–
    White Bead Ceremony / by Sherrin Watkins: illustrated by Kim Doner.
    p. cm.— (The Greyfeather series)
  Summary: Mary Greyfeather experiences the traditional Shawnee ceremony
by which children are given a tribal name.
    ISBN 0-933031-92-0: $16.95, — ISBN 0-933031-26-2
    1. Shawnee Indians– Rites and ceremonies– Juvenile fiction.
[1. Shawnee Indians– Rites and ceremonies— Fiction.   2. Indians of
North America—Rites and ceremonies—Fiction.] I. Doner, Kim, 1955–   ill.
II. Title. III. Series: Watkins, Sherrin, 1954–   Greyfeather series.
PZ7.W315Wh 1994
[Fic]– dc20
    93-50735
    CIP
    AC

ISBN 0-933031-92-0

ISBN 0-933031-26-2, *The Greyfeather Series*

PRONUNCIATION KEY

The letters in the Shawnee words in the text have the following values:

A	as in "hay"
E	as in "see"
I	as in "pin"
O	as in "mole"
G	always hard as in "give"
R	as aw in "paw"
OO	as in "took"
U	as in "luck"
P	as in English
C	"tsi", similar to ch in "chin"
TH	as in "the"
H	as in English but it can also be silent after a consonant, signifying a short silence or aspirant pause.
J	as in "jail"
K, L, M, N, S, T, W	all as in English
Y	as in "yes"

$\mathcal{W}$hat's this?" Mary's Momma asked her, holding up a picture of a housecat.

"I want to play Barbies," said Mary looking at her feet.

"First, say '*posethu*,' cat."

Mary just stared at her feet some more.

"What do we live in? Say '*wegiwu*,' house. Say '*wegiwu*,' Mary."

"I want to play Barbies," said Mary again.

"All right," Momma sighed, "go play."

"I just want to be English," Mary said turning to go.

"When all the old Shawnee people who talk this talk are gone forever, there will still be more English here than there are stars in the sky at night, Mary. You think about that!"

"No one wants to play with Maria Menendez because she's not English. She only talks Spanish," said Mary as she left the room.

house
wegiwu

cat
posethu

mother
nigiu

"*Ni Dawnaytha*, my daughter," said Momma to Mary's Grandma.

Grandma said, "If you're angry and impatient with her, she'll be an angry, impatient person."

"She won't learn!" said Momma. "She's old enough to know Shawnee words."

"Mary is learning all the time," Grandma said. "What are you teaching her? You tell her a few words, then get angry when she doesn't want to know them."

"Don't you want her to know Shawnee language?" asked Momma.

"I want her to know lots of things. She's four years old and doesn't even have a Shawnee name," Grandma scolded.

"We lived in Texas when she was born. There aren't any Shawnee people in Texas to help name a baby," Momma answered.

"You're not in Texas now," said Grandma. "Call your husband's Aunt Jennie and my sister Lenexa and ask them to bring names this Saturday for Mary. My sister Laura won't do to name Mary because two of her own children have died. That would be bad luck for Mary. Laura can bring the white-bead necklace for Mary to wear when she gets her name. You fix the food. I'll call and invite our relatives and friends."

"That's a lot of people to cook for," said Momma.

"That's your job," said Grandma. "Besides, everyone will bring something."

On Saturday Mary's grandmothers woke her up and washed her face and arms with warm, wet washcloths. It tickled and she giggled.

"You're going to get a white-bead necklace today, Mary," said Grandma Greyfeather.

"You put it on with your name and you wear it until it wears out," said Grandma Spybuck.

"I wore mine two years until I lost it playing," Grandma Greyfeather told her.

"Esther, I want you to know, I've still got mine. My mother saved it for me after the string broke," said Grandma Spybuck.

All the time, Mary heard voices as Grandma Greyfeather and Grandma Spybuck helped her dress in her best pink Sunday dress and her lace anklets and her white patent leather shoes she got last Easter. Grandma Spybuck brushed Mary's mink-colored hair and Grandma Greyfeather tied a pink bow on her ponytail.

When they finished Mary went into the living room and sat on Momma's lap and tried to act like all those noisy people weren't there to see her.

"Does anyone have extra Polaroid films?" asked Uncle George.

Grandma Spybuck said, "Laura's bringing some."

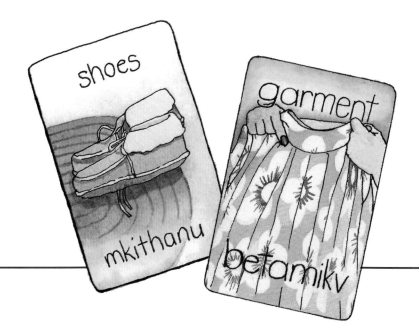

shoes
mkithanu

garment
betamikv

Eleven year old Billy Exendine piped up, "That was her on the phone a while ago. Her car's broke down. She can't make it."

"What!" exclaimed Grandma Greyfeather.

"She's got the necklace!" said Grandma Spybuck.

"Why didn't you tell someone she called?" asked Billy's mother.

Everyone got quiet. They all looked at Mary on Momma's lap.

"Joe," said Grandma Greyfeather, "take me to Jane's sewing room. Don't worry Jane," she said to Momma, "your Mary will have a necklace. Go ahead and get started. We'll be right back."

The old ladies, Jennie Exendine and Lenexa Bluejacket stood up.

Great Aunt Jennie talked first. "My nephew Joe's wife –you all know Jane– called me and asked me to name their child, Mary. She also called her mother's sister, Lenexa Bluejacket here, and asked her to bring a name today for Mary. We've studied this matter very carefully and thought about all kinds of animals and their names because that's how old ladies like us are supposed to do this."

"Who's an old lady?" chimed in Great Aunt Lenexa. Her two white braids were twisted in knots on either side of her head. "Ninety's not so old," she said to Mary swaying slightly in her cotton wash dress and freshly-bleached white cloth shoes.

Because she spoke Shawnee a long time before she learned English, she said "ah" instead of "r", and made "wuh" noises instead of "v" and "f" sounds when she talked English. "I'm not a bumblebee," she'd say when her family laughed at her for not being able to make "z" sounds.

Uncle George set a chair beside her for her to lean on.

"Anyway," she said, "we've prayed about bird names, *pelee womhsoomi*, about turtle and water-life names, *kahkilee womhsoomi*, and rounded-feet animal names, *petekothitee womhsoomi*. That's like dog, wolf, ones with rounded paws here." She showed the palm of her hand.

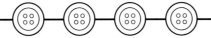

Aunt Jennie joined in. "We thought about them before we slept and Mrs. Bluejacket here even dreamed about animals and their names."

Aunt Lenexa Bluejacket went on. "We thought about the leaf-eaters, the grass-eaters, what we call horse-name animals, *mseewi womhsoomi*. We thought about claw-footed animals like raccoon and bear, *thepati womhsoomi*. Last, we turned our minds to rabbit-name animals, *petakineethi womhsoomi*, because those have a peaceful, gentle nature."

Mary's cousins were beginning to whisper too loud. They fidgeted and giggled at the way Great Aunt Lenexa talked when she said, leaf-eaters– "leaw eates" –and grass eaters– "gass eates."

"Gas! She said 'gas'," hooted Billy Exendine, just before his mother took him out of the room.

"What have you decided?" asked Momma.

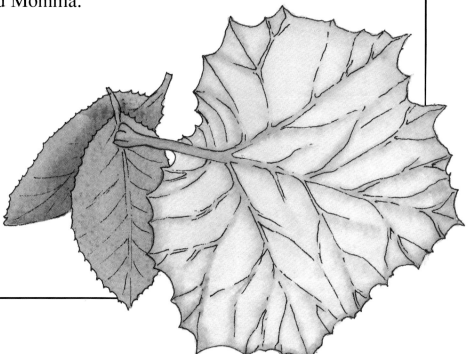

Great Aunt Jennie smiled at Mary. "Well a name has to fit a person and I know our Mary likes to swim. I know all the animals are wonderful but turtle-name animals and those that swim are strong and graceful. These animals have always been helpful to people, feeding us, sustaining us, delighting us. They are pretty and curious. They tend to have lovely markings on their bodies. There is something wise and stately about these animals. And let's not forget that some of the swimmers are very fast."

The children settled down when Jennie began to talk about animals. "Ladies and Gentlemen," Jennie said looking at them, "I bring Mary the name *Mayataykamshi*, one who rests back in odd waters."

Mary giggled.

"What name would you give Mary?" Momma asked old Lenexa Bluejacket.

"Fishes and turtles and all swimmers are fine, regal creatures. But I prayed about this too and I had a dream of horses. These horses were beautiful and fast, to take a person with joy and strength and speed through life."

The children were very quiet now, watching the old woman.

"Horse-name animals like deer and elk and buffalo used to be very important to Shawnee for food and clothes before we began trading for cotton cloth a long time ago. So horse-name animals are friendly, hard-working, beautiful, or helpful creatures. So that's why I bring the name *Wapapiyeshe* for Mary."

Mary's dad and Grandma Greyfeather came back into the room. You could tell they had been hurrying.

Aunt Lenexa continued, "That means, white-necked, moving."

Momma said, "I like that one."

Mary's dad said, "Then it's a good one."

Mary went and stood by Great Aunt Lenexa Bluejacket who said, "It is the rule of the Creator, God– Shawnee say '*Maneto*'– that we name a child within ten days of its birth. But Maneto knows times have changed for Shawnee people, and that's why we are here today. It's still important for Shawnee to say we are glad to have this girl this morning.

deer
psagthe

elk
wrpiti

buffalo
mthothwu

girl
sgwuhthathu

woman
ikwawu

grandmother
huhkumihimu

"Lots of people think a girl like this doesn't know anything or mean much, but we think this girl knows more than we do because she was with God– Maneto– more recently than we were. And it was Maneto that sent her to us, like Maneto sent the animals that we live with, that help us, that we get names from to carry us through our lives.

"These animals are fast, or smart, or strong, or sociable, or lovely, like we want to be in our lives. That's why we take our names from them. That's why I found a horse-name for this girl, and that's what I'm giving her now."

Mary sat down with her Momma again.

"Some day she will be a woman, helping us, feeding us when we visit, just as we are helping her and feasting her today. In those days, when I am gone, and she is grown, this name I give her today will have carried her a long way.

"First, she is a girl, then she is a young woman, then she will be an old grandma, like me. This name will take her that far– a long way."

"Everybody will call her, *Wapapiyeshe*," the old woman said as Mary's Grandma Greyfeather helped her tie something around Mary's neck.

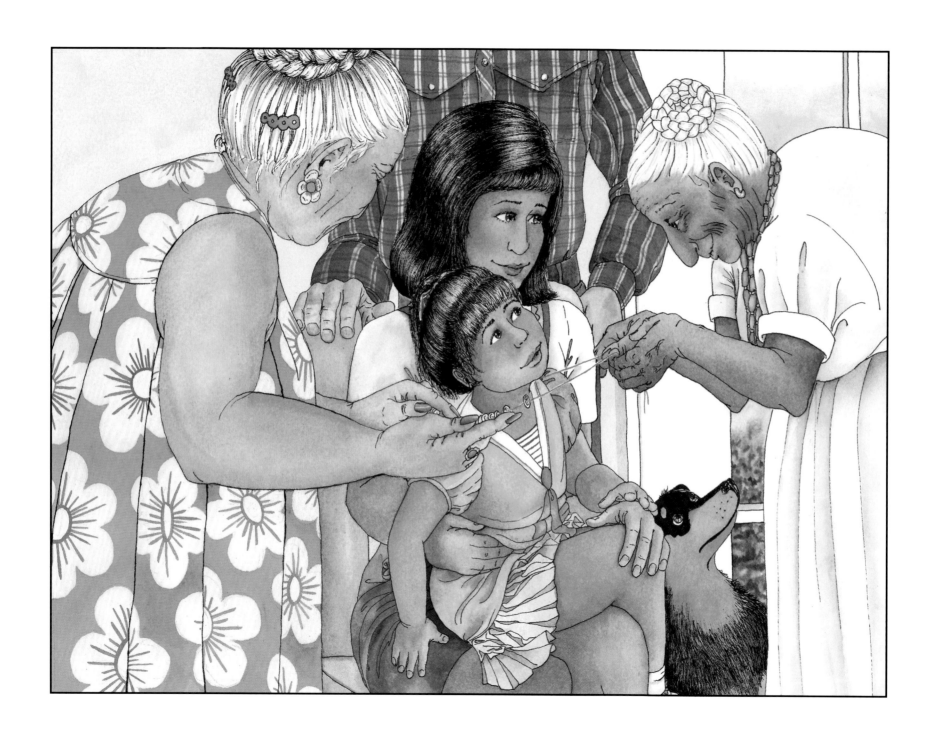

Mary looked at it. It was a hundred beautiful white buttons, all sizes and shapes, from Momma's button box, threaded onto a string of dental floss.

"Yes," Lenexa said, "that's what everyone will call her– Wapapiyeshe."

"From now on, she will be called Wapapiyeshe," and a fourth time she spoke it. "Everyone all the time will say Wapapiyeshe."

Grandma Spybuck said, "Let's eat with Wapapiyeshe this morning."

Momma said, "You have a good name Wapapiyeshe. Thank you for that name Lenexa."

white-necked, moving
wapapiyeshe

Mary hugged both her old aunties, then they all ate eggs scrambled with wild green onions picked and cleaned and frozen for just such an occasion. They ate bacon, and biscuits with gravy, and fried potatoes, and corn bread.

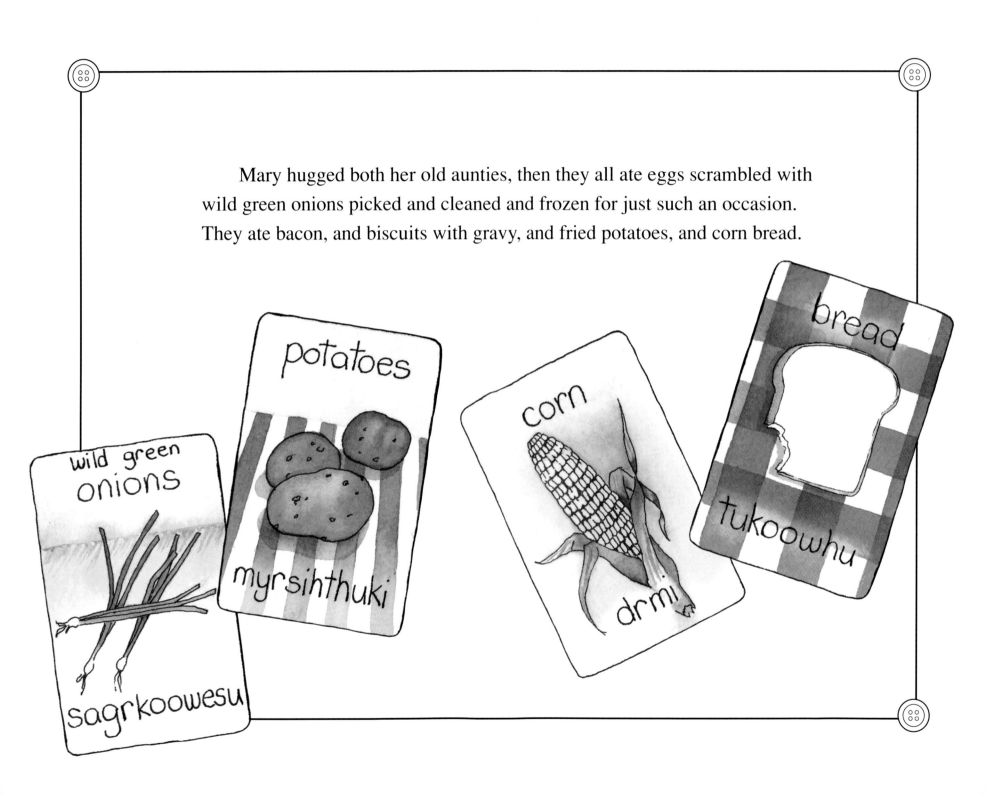

wild green
onions

sagrkoowesu

potatoes

myrsihthuki

corn

drmi

bread

tukoowhu

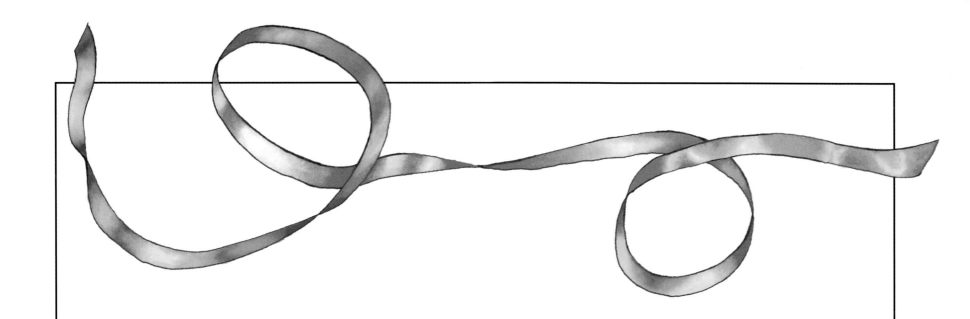

After breakfast Grandma Spybuck gave Mary a bottle of soap bubbles.
"For Wapapiyeshe," she said as she handed the gift to her.

The others took turns handing her presents, a Barbie doll, a bottle of
Jergen's lotion, each one saying: "I bought this for you, Wapapiyeshe," or
"We're glad to have you, Wapapiyeshe," or "Pleased to meet you,
Wapapiyeshe."

After everyone went home, Mary sat with her Grandpa Spybuck. She had pulled her button necklace up and put it in her mouth.

"Look here, she's trying to button her lip," Grandpa teased. "What's that name again? Wapapiwhatsis?"

Mary giggled.

"That's my name group too," he said, "horse-name group."

"What's your name, Grandpa?"

"I am *Wapamiyepto*, running on a white path."

"Pleased to meet you, *Wapamiyepto*,"
said Mary laughing.

SHAWNEE HISTORY

Once Shawnee Indians lived in Kentucky, Ohio, Illinois, and Indiana. They lived in villages. Their houses were made from the bark of trees. Their houses looked like small cabins. Shawnee grew corn and hunted deer to eat. They made clothes from deerskins.

There were five tribes of Shawnee. They were called *Chalakathu, Kispokogee, Hathawakilu, Makujay,* and *Pekoowethu.* Shawnee villages were often named for the largest Shawnee tribe that lived there. There are still towns today called Chillicothe and Piqua after the Shawnee who once lived there.

Shawnee say Delaware Indians are their grandfathers. They say this because they like Delaware people so much. Shawnee say Kickapoo Indians are really Shawnee Indians who had to leave their people after they stole some bear paws.

Shawnee language is Algonquin. That means Shawnee language is related to the languages of other Indians. Some of the tribes which have languages related to Shawnee are Delaware, Sac and Fox, Kickapoo, Potawatomi, Chippewa, Cheyenne, and Arapaho.

Shawnee people liked to visit their friends. Many Shawnee lived with other Indians. Some Shawnee lived with Seneca Indians. Some lived with Euchee Indians. Some lived with Tuckabatchee Indians.

Once a Shawnee man named Tecumthu wanted all the Indian people to join together to fight the white people. Tecumthu's brother was called Prophet by English-speaking people. His Shawnee name meant "Open Door."

Tecumthu's brother taught Indians that they must return to their old ways. He said Indians must give up everything they learned from white people.

Many Indians believe that a terrible earthquake which shook the United States was caused when Tecumthu stomped his foot. Tecumthu was killed fighting for his beliefs.

Today there are Shawnee people living with the Cherokee in Oklahoma. There are Eastern Shawnee people in Oklahoma too.

They are the Shawnee who used to live with the Seneca. Some Shawnee live around the town of Shawnee, Oklahoma. They are called Absentee Shawnee.

I hope you always enjoy reading about Shawnee people.

✂ Cut along lines

✂ Cut along lines

white-necked, moving

wapapiyeshe

father

nioohthu

running on a white path

wapamiyepto

potatoes

myrsihthuki

horse

msawa

mother

nigiu

otter

gituta

dog

wihsi

✂ Cut along lines ✂

girl

sgwuhthathu

sun

inugesagi

rabbit

petakenethu

fish

numahthu

corn

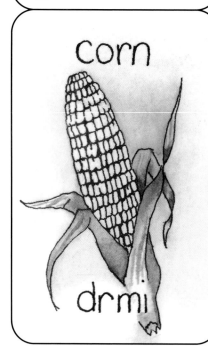

drmi

elk

wrpiti

man

ilani

raccoon

ithaputi

✂ Cut along lines ✂

✄ Cut along lines ✄

woman
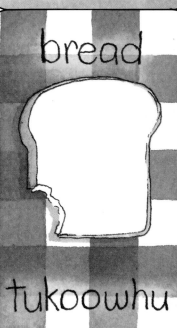
ikwawu

turkey

palawu

wild green
onions
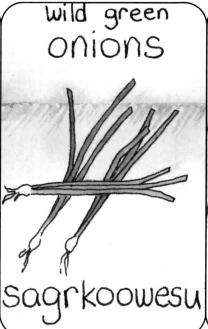
sagrkoowesu

wolf

ptweowa

bread

tukoowhu

buffalo

mthothwu

cup

tiphikuh

grandmother

huhkumthimu

✄ Cut along lines ✄

cat

posethu

house

wegiwu

bird

wiskelothu

canoe

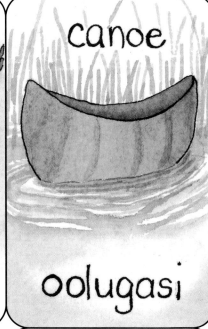

oolugasi

beaver

umahgwu

bear

mookwu

shoes

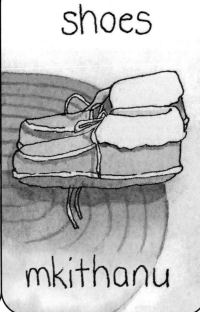

mkithanu

deer

psagthe

Cut along lines

Cut along lines